D1529881

J   970360
2nd
GLENDINNING   Glendinning, Sally
               Jimmy and Joe find
               a ghost

DATE DUE

MAY 29 2007			
JUN 1 8 2007			
AUG 2 0 2007			

Jimmy and Joe Find a Ghost

Jimmy and Joe Find a GHOST

by Sally Glendinning

paintings by Paul Frame

book design: Ted Schroeder

GARRARD PUBLISHING COMPANY

CHAMPAIGN, ILLINOIS

Jimmy and Joe
Find a Ghost

"What can we do today?"
Jimmy asked Joe.
Joe put down his book.
"Let's do something new,"
Joe said.
"Let's look for a ghost!"

"Maybe a ghost lives
in our tree-house,"
said Jimmy.
"Let's look!" said Joe.
The boys climbed
up the big tree.
They saw a squirrel
eating a nut.
They saw a blue bird
sitting in her nest.
"There's no ghost up here,"
said Jimmy.
"Let's look in the woods,"
said Joe.

The boys climbed down
from the tree-house.
They walked to the woods.
They saw a brown rabbit
and a red fox.
They saw a green frog
and a yellow duck.

"Do you see a ghost?"
asked Jimmy.
"No," said Joe.
"Maybe the ghost
lives in a house."

The boys walked
to an old, old house.
There was no door.
The windows were broken.
"Let's go in," said Joe.
"All right," Jimmy said.

"A ghost wouldn't live
in this old house,"
said Jimmy.
"There's a cat!" cried Joe.
"MEOW!" went the cat.
Then a mouse ran by.

The cat wanted
to catch the mouse.
The mouse ran away.
Jimmy and Joe laughed.
Then they sat down
in two broken chairs.
"No ghost lives
in this old house,"
said Joe.
"Mr. Jones has a new house,"
said Jimmy.
"Maybe a ghost lives there.
If I were a ghost,
I'd live in a new house."

The boys ran down the street
to Mr. Jones' store.
They found Mr. Jones.
"Good morning!" he called.
"Here is a big red apple
for each of you."

"May we look for a ghost
in your new house?"
asked Jimmy.
"A ghost!" said Mr. Jones.
"There isn't a ghost there.
But you can look if you want."

Jimmy and Joe ran
to the new house.
The door was open.
"Come on, Jimmy," said Joe.
"All right," said Jimmy.
They went into the house.

They saw a table and chairs
and boxes of books.
"This is a pretty room,"
said Jimmy.
"But I don't see a ghost."
Then they heard a noise.
"What was that?" asked Joe.

Then SOMETHING went
flippety-flop, flippety-flop,
flippety-flop.
"It must be a ghost,"
cried Jimmy.
A blue chair came flying
from the hall.
"Wow!" yelled Joe.
"That's a bad ghost!"
The ghost made a noise again.
Flippety-flop, flippety-flop,
flippety-flop.
"I'm scared," said Jimmy.
"So am I," said Joe.

Jimmy and Joe tiptoed
into another room.
The boys looked around.
In the room was a big bed.
"Let's hide!" whispered Jimmy.
"Let's hide under the bed,"
whispered Joe.

The boys hid under the bed.
They could see the door.
A big red ball
rolled into the room.
"Maybe the ghost
wants to play ball with us,"
whispered Jimmy.

"I don't want to play ball,"
whispered Joe.
"I want to go home."
"Let's go home now,"
said Jimmy.
The boys came out
from under the bed.
They saw something
big and brown
go by the door.
It began to climb the steps.
Flippety-flop, flippety-flop.
"It has on a fur coat,"
whispered Jimmy.

"A ghost in a fur coat!"
whispered Joe.
It was quiet for a minute.
It was quiet for another minute.
Then a yellow box
bumped down the steps.
"That bad ghost!" cried Jimmy.
They could hear the ghost.
It was moving about.
Flippety-flop, flippety-flop.
There was a new noise.
Splash. Splash. Splash.
"That's water running,"
said Joe.

Then SOMETHING went
splash, splash, splash.
"The ghost is taking a bath,"
whispered Jimmy.
Water began to run
down the steps.
"My shoes are wet," said Joe.
"So are mine," said Jimmy.
Jimmy looked at Joe.
"What shall we do?" he asked.
"That bad old ghost
will hurt this new house!"
"We must go up there," said Joe.
"I guess so," said Jimmy.

Jimmy and Joe tiptoed
up the steps.
They were very scared.
They could hear the ghost
splashing in the water.
"AH-h-h," cried the ghost.

"Look out!" cried Jimmy.
A cake of green soap
came flying at them.
The soap hit Joe's head.
Then came a toy boat.
The boat hit Jimmy's head.

Jimmy and Joe climbed
to the top of the steps.
They walked to the door
of the bathroom.
"That ghost may hurt us,"
whispered Joe.

Just then the ghost
made a BIG SPLASH!
The boys got wet
from head to toe.
"Let's catch that ghost!"
cried Jimmy and Joe.

Now the boys were angry.
They were so angry
that they forgot to be scared.
They walked into the bathroom
side by side.
Then they began to laugh.
The ghost in the fur coat
was in the bathtub.
It was big and brown.
But it wasn't a ghost at all.
"Our ghost is a seal!"
shouted Jimmy.
"Why, it's Susie the seal
from the zoo," laughed Joe.

Susie went flippety-flop,
flippety-flop, flippety-flop.
She was happy to see the boys.
"Is Susie stuck in the tub?"
asked Joe.
"Oh, no," said Jimmy.
"Susie can climb out
if she wants to."

But Susie didn't want
to get out of the tub.
"Come now, Susie," said Jimmy.
Susie splashed more.
"I'll ask Mr. Jones
to come here and help us,"
said Joe.

Soon Mr. Jones
came back with Joe.
With them was a man
from the zoo.
The man had a pail of fish.
"Susie ran away," he said.
"I must find her."
They went up to the bathroom
where Susie sat in the tub.
The man held a fish
near Susie's nose.
Susie wanted that fish.
She went flippety-flop
and jumped out of the tub.

Susie ate the fish.
Then she wanted more.
Mr. Jones and the boys
and the man from the zoo
went down the steps.
Flippety-flop, flippety-flop.
Down the steps came Susie.

Susie looked at the fish.
She wanted more fish.
The man put the fish in his car,
and Susie climbed in after them.
Then she put her head
out of the window.
She looked at the boys.

"There goes your ghost,"
Mr. Jones said to the boys.
Jimmy and Joe laughed.
"Now we have a ghost story
to tell at school,"
said Jimmy.
"Susie is our ghost," said Joe.